The Rooftop Rocket Party

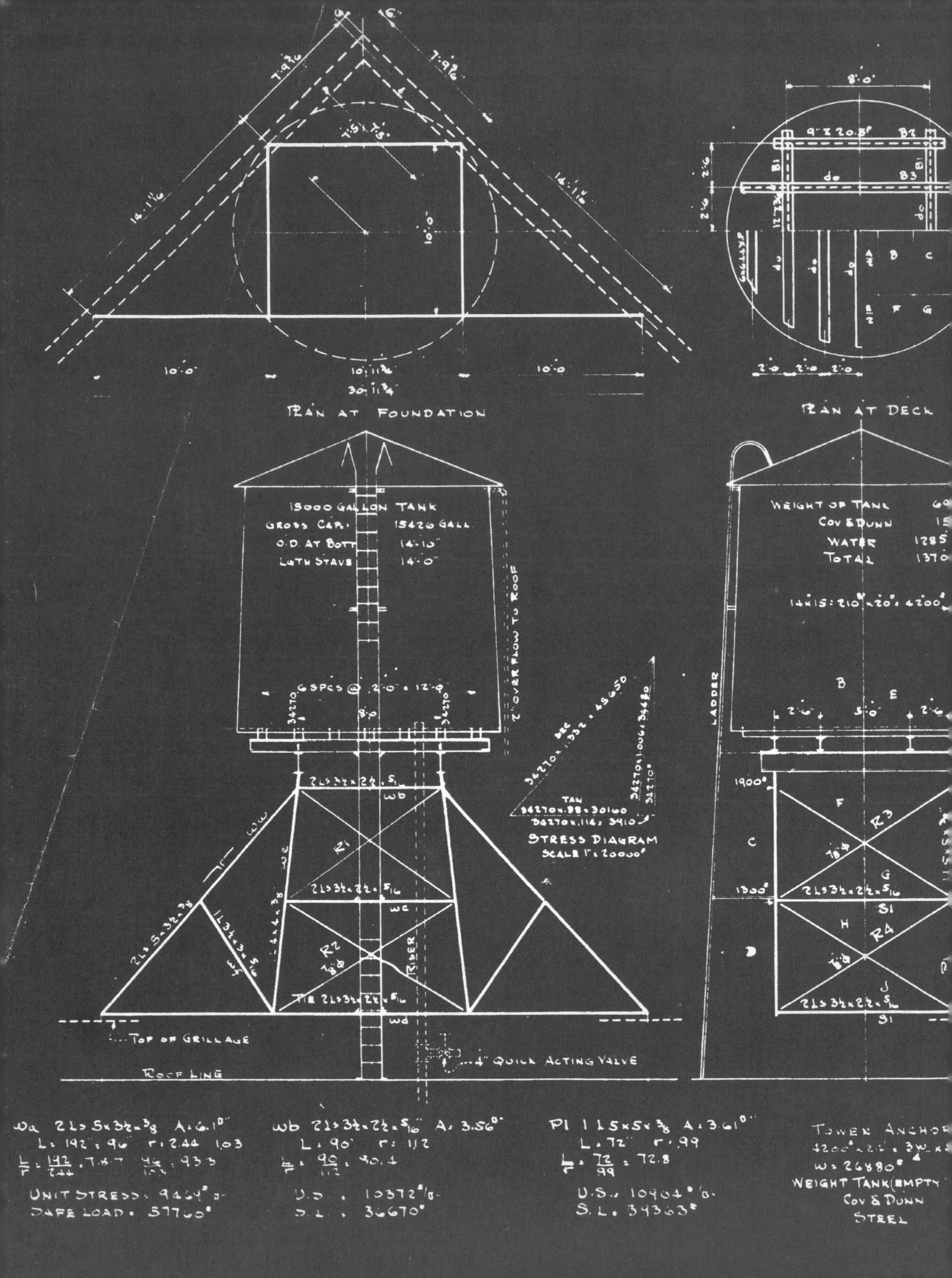

PLAN AT FOUNDATION
PLAN AT DECK
15000 GALLON TANK
GROSS CAP. 15426 GALL.
O.D. AT BOTT 14-10"
LGTH STAVE 14-0"
WEIGHT OF TANK
COV & DUNN
WATER
TOTAL
4" OVERFLOW TO ROOF
LADDER
STRESS DIAGRAM
SCALE 1" = 20000#
RISER
TOP OF GRILLAGE
ROOF LINE
4" QUICK ACTING VALVE
UNIT STRESS = 9464#/□"
SAFE LOAD = 57760#
U.S. = 10372#/□"
S.L. = 36670#
U.S. = 10404#/□"
S.L. = 34363#
TOWER ANCHOR
W = 26880#
WEIGHT TANK (EMPTY
COV & DUNN
STEEL

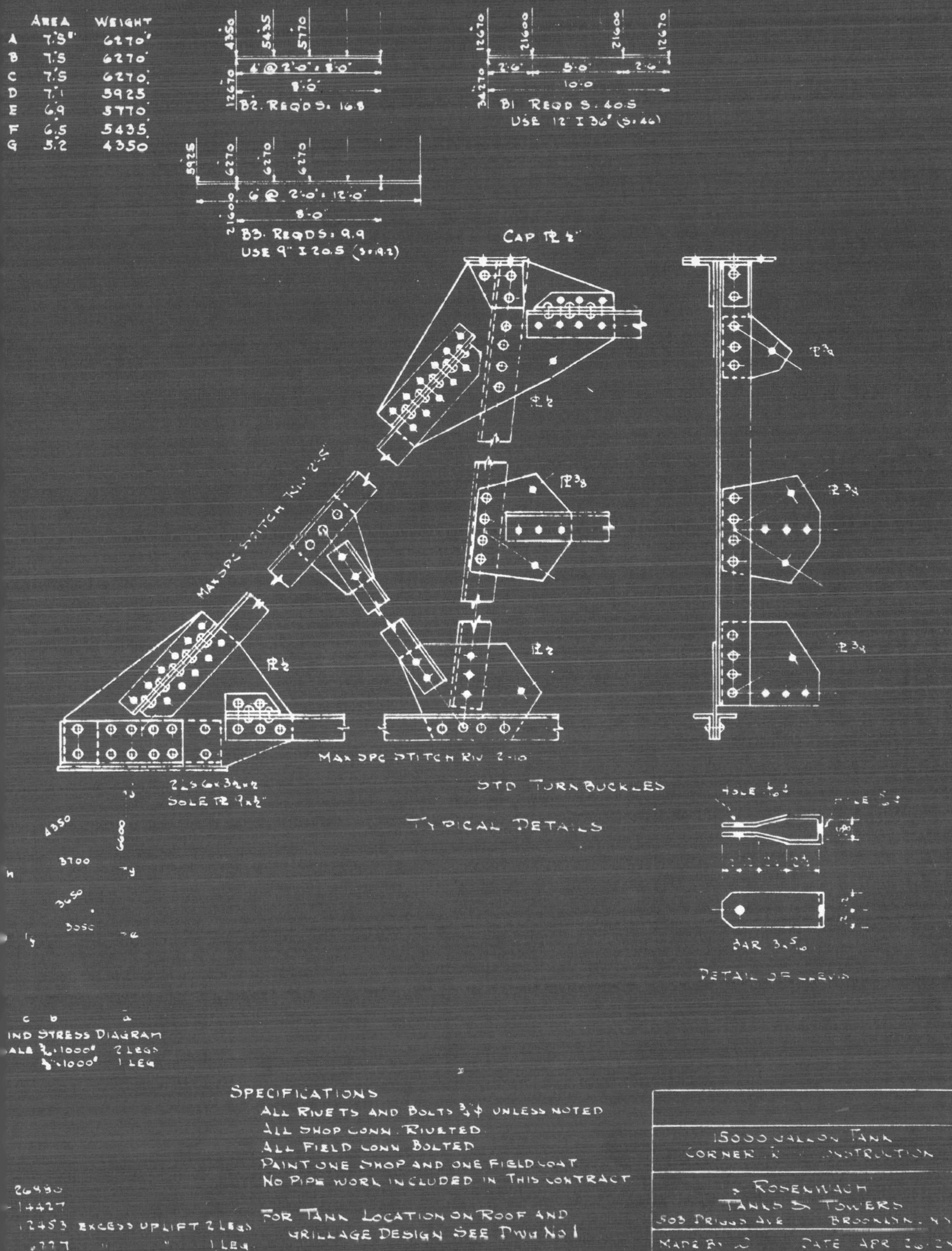
AREA WEIGHT
A 7.5" 6270'
B 7.5 6270
C 7.5 6270
D 7.1 5925
E 6.9 5770
F 6.5 5435
G 5.2 4350
6 @ 2'-0" = 8'-0"
8'-0"
B2. REQD S. 16.8
2'-6" 5'-0" 2'-6"
10'-0"
B1 REQD S. 40.5
USE 12" I 36' (S. 46)
6 @ 2'-0" = 12'-0"
8'-0"
B3. REQDS. 9.9
USE 9" I 20.5 (S. 19.2)
CAP
MAX SPC STITCH RIV 2'-5"
MAX SPC STITCH RIV 2'-10
STD TURNBUCKLES
TYPICAL DETAILS
BAR
DETAIL OF CLEVIS
WIND STRESS DIAGRAM
SPECIFICATIONS
ALL RIVETS AND BOLTS 3/4" φ UNLESS NOTED
ALL SHOP CONN. RIVETED
ALL FIELD CONN. BOLTED
PAINT ONE SHOP AND ONE FIELD COAT
NO PIPE WORK INCLUDED IN THIS CONTRACT
FOR TANK LOCATION ON ROOF AND GRILLAGE DESIGN SEE DWG NO 1
26880
- 14427
12453 EXCESS UPLIFT 2 LEGS
1 LEG
USE NOT LESS THAN
3/4" φ BOLTS
15000 GALLON TANK
CORNER ... CONSTRUCTION
ROSENWACH
TANKS & TOWERS
503 DRIGGS AVE BROOKLYN, N.Y.
MADE BY DATE APR
CHKED BY DATE
DRAWING NO. 15CT1 JOB NO

Many thanks to the Rosenwach family
for providing blueprints of the water towers,
and for building them—R.C.

The Rooftop Rocket Party

Roland Chambers

A
Andersen Press
London

In the summer, Finn went to visit Doctor Gass in New York.

Doctor Gass was a famous Rocket Scientist.

But when Finn asked Doctor Gass where he *kept* his rockets, the brilliant man just smiled and said:

"In a very secret and unusual place."

There were no proper rockets in Doctor Gass's laboratory, which was green and full of plans.

Or in his library, which was red and full of books.

There were no rockets at all in Central Park, though Finn thought it would make a fantastic Launch Pad.

And although there were plenty in the Museum of Rocket Science, none of them belonged to Doctor Gass.

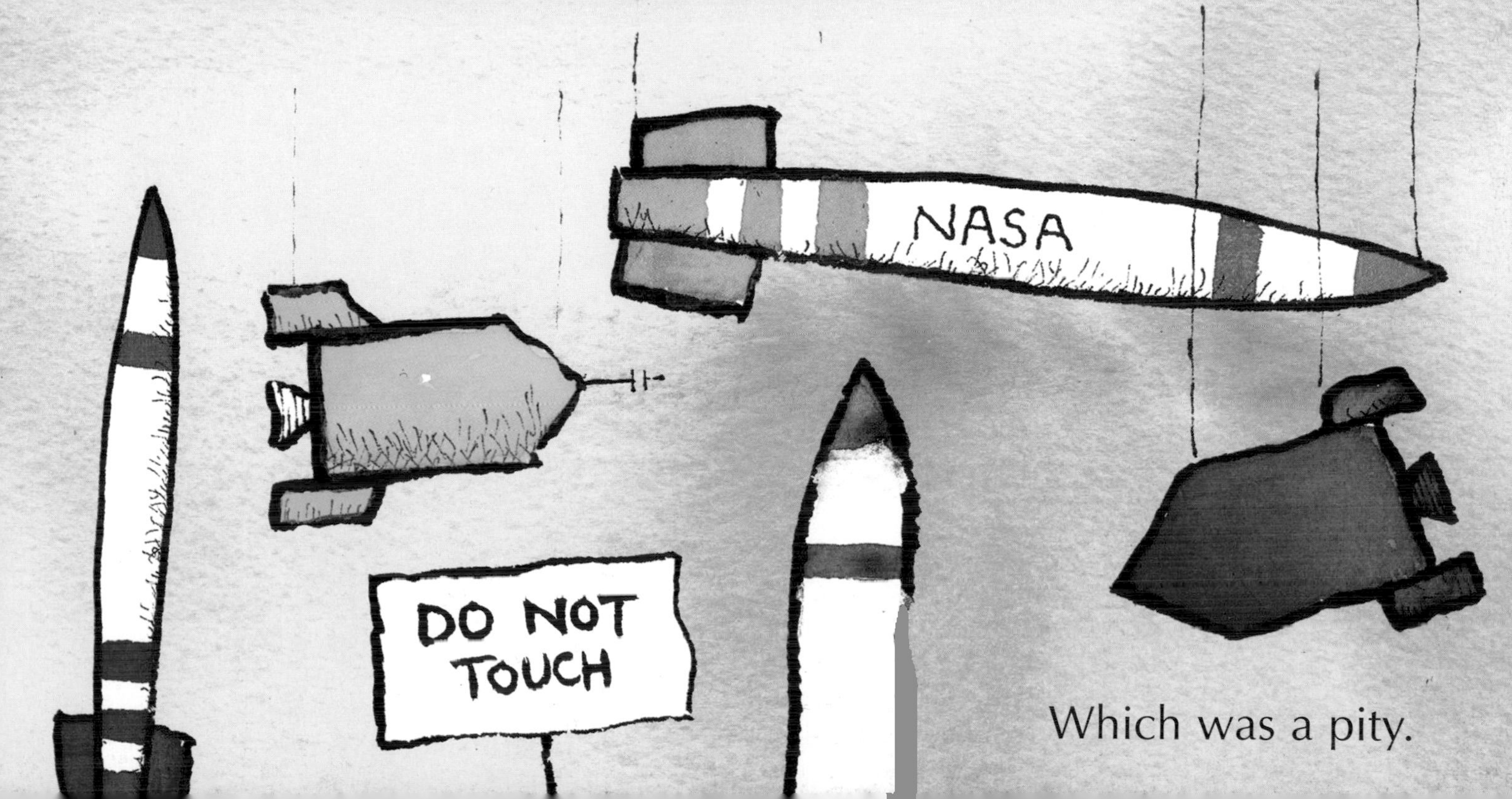

Which was a pity.

That evening, over supper, Doctor Gass explained to Finn how the Moon moved around the Earth and was made of rocks.

“I always thought the Moon was made of cheese,” said Finn.
“The Moon is a stone,” said Doctor Gass.
“Then what does the Man in the Moon eat for his supper?” wondered Finn.
“There is no supper on the Moon,” said Doctor Gass, “and what is more there is no Man in the Moon to eat it.”
“Is that so?” said Finn.
“That,” replied Doctor Gass, “is a mathematical certainty.”

“Oh,” said Finn . . .

. . . and went to bed.

But at twelve o'clock, when everybody was asleep, a Night Thing came tapping at his window.
"Good evening," said the Night Thing. "My master is the Man in the Moon and he has asked me to invite you to his birthday party."

"But Doctor Gass says there is no Man in the Moon," said Finn.
"Is that so?" said the Night Thing.
"That," said Finn, "is a mathematical certainty."
The Night Thing just yawned and licked his chops.

"Twelve o'clock tomorrow night," he said, "don't be late."

The next morning Finn told Doctor Gass what he had seen.

"But that was just a dream!" said Doctor Gass.

And he explained how dreams worked.

And went on explaining until Finn begged him to stop.

That day they climbed the Empire State Building, which was tall, but not *that* tall.

"How far away is the Moon?" asked Finn.
"The Moon," replied Doctor Gass,
"is 240,000 miles away."
"A long way," said Finn.
"An *amazingly* long way," said Doctor Gass.

"Oh dear," said Finn . . .

. . . and climbed down again.

But on the way home he saw something that made him point and shout, "Doctor Gass! I know where you hide your rockets!"

And there, on the rooftops, were big, red rockets, ready for lift-off!

"But those aren't rockets," laughed Doctor Gass, "they're water towers!"

And he explained how water towers held water to drink, and to shower and to wash dishes now and then.

And he went on explaining until Finn begged him to stop.

That evening, Finn asked Doctor Gass where he *did* keep his rockets.

"My rockets?" replied Doctor Gass, "Why, I keep them in the most secret and unusual place of all . . .

. . . my *head!!*"

Finn was so disappointed that he went to bed without touching his supper . . .

. . . which wasn't like Finn at all.

But at five minutes to twelve the Night Thing came tapping at his window.

"Hurry!" he said.
"No time to dress . . ."

Up on the roof stood
the red tower.

"Just remember," said the Night
Thing, "every child in New York
has a rocket on his rooftop."

Lift-off!

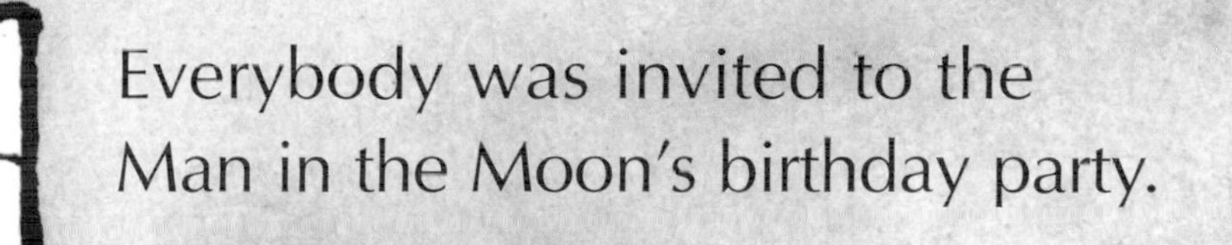

Everybody was invited to the
Man in the Moon's birthday party.

When they landed,
the Man in the Moon met
them one by one.

"Good night!" he said,
"and welcome . . ."

"And now,
let the fun begin!"

First they played the
bouncing game.

Finn bounced so high he
thought he'd never come
down again.

Next they hunted each other through
the moon caves, which were all
lit up with green.

When they were hungry they
had a picnic. . .

. . . which tasted like nothing on Earth.

"But where is the cheese?" wondered Finn.

"I am sorry," replied the Man in the Moon, "I have eaten all the cheese. Please have a meringue."

And then . . .

. . . when they were all sleepy . . .

. . . and the night was almost over . . .

. . . the Man in the Moon
played them a tune on his
pale violin.

And then it was time to go home.

The next morning Doctor Gass went
into his bathroom to brush his teeth.

But there was no water in the tap. Not a drop.

So he went outside in his
dressing gown to investigate.

And there he saw something so unmathematical . . .

. . . so *very* unscientific . . .

. . . that he closed his eyes and said, "RIDICULOUS!"

It was a great red rocket parked right in the middle of the street!

And close by, on the sidewalk,
was a half-eaten meringue . . .

. . . which belonged to a little boy
who was fast asleep upstairs . . .

. . . because space travel
is very exhausting.

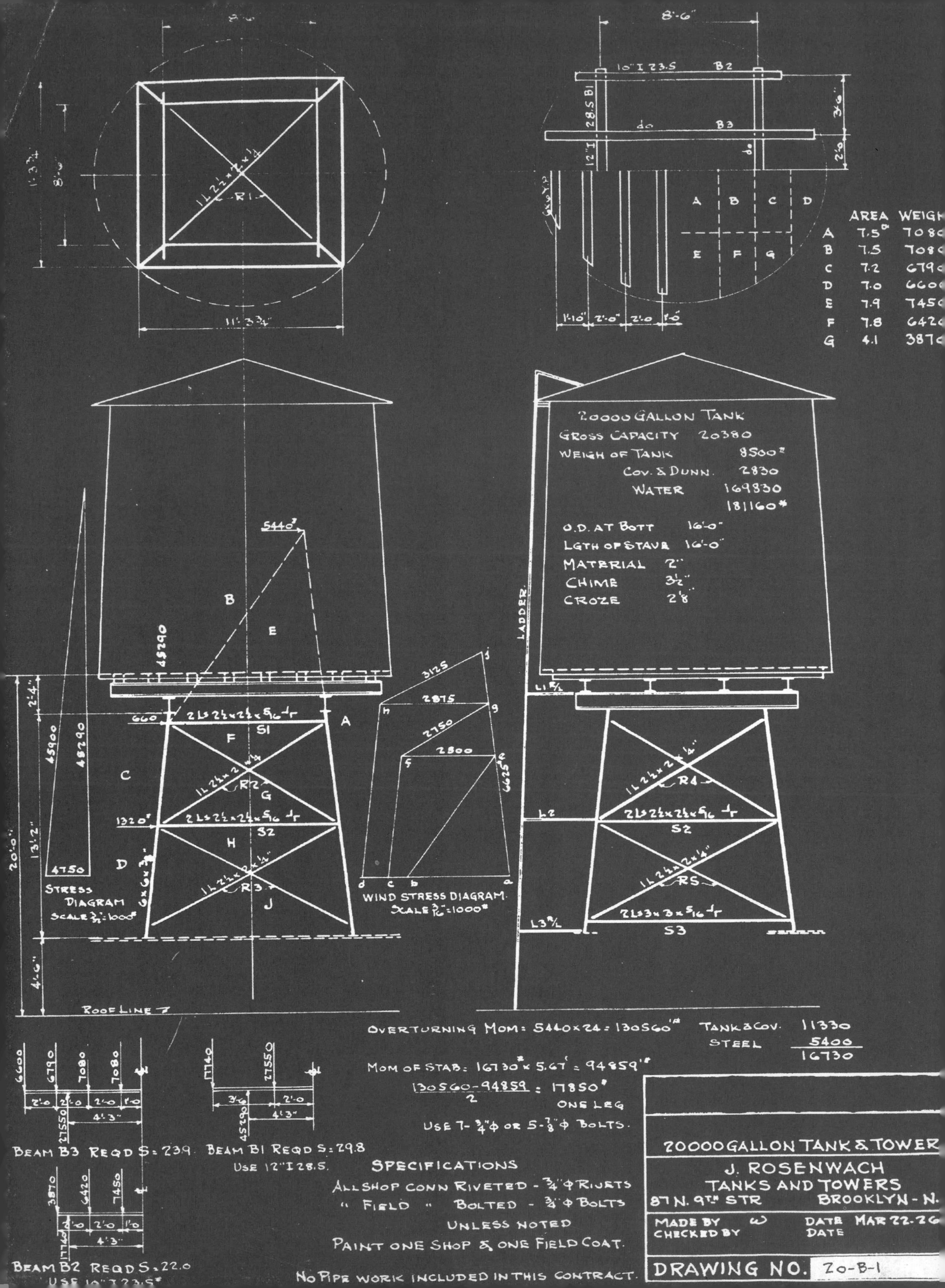

20000 GALLON TANK
GROSS CAPACITY 20380
WEIGH OF TANK 8500#
COV. & DUNN. 2830
WATER 169830
181160#
O.D. AT BOTT 16'-0"
LGTH OF STAVE 16'-0"
MATERIAL 2"
CHIME 3½"
CROZE 2⅛"
AREA WEIGH
A 7.5 708
B 7.5 708
C 7.2 679
D 7.0 660
E 7.9 745
F 7.8 642
G 4.1 387
STRESS DIAGRAM
WIND STRESS DIAGRAM
LADDER
ROOF LINE
OVERTURNING MOM: 5440×24 = 130560"#
TANK & COV. 11330
STEEL 5400
16730
MOM OF STAB: 16730# × 5.67' = 94859"#
130560-94859 / 2 = 17850#
ONE LEG
USE 7-¾"φ OR 5-⅞"φ BOLTS.
BEAM B3 REQD S = 23.9
BEAM B1 REQD S = 29.8
USE 12"I 28.5
BEAM B2 REQD S = 22.0
SPECIFICATIONS
ALL SHOP CONN RIVETED - ¾"φ RIVETS
" FIELD " BOLTED - ¾"φ BOLTS
UNLESS NOTED
PAINT ONE SHOP & ONE FIELD COAT.
NO PIPE WORK INCLUDED IN THIS CONTRACT.
20000 GALLON TANK & TOWER
J. ROSENWACH
TANKS AND TOWERS
87 N. 9TH STR
BROOKLYN - N.
MADE BY
CHECKED BY
DATE MAR 22-26
DATE
DRAWING NO. 20-B-1

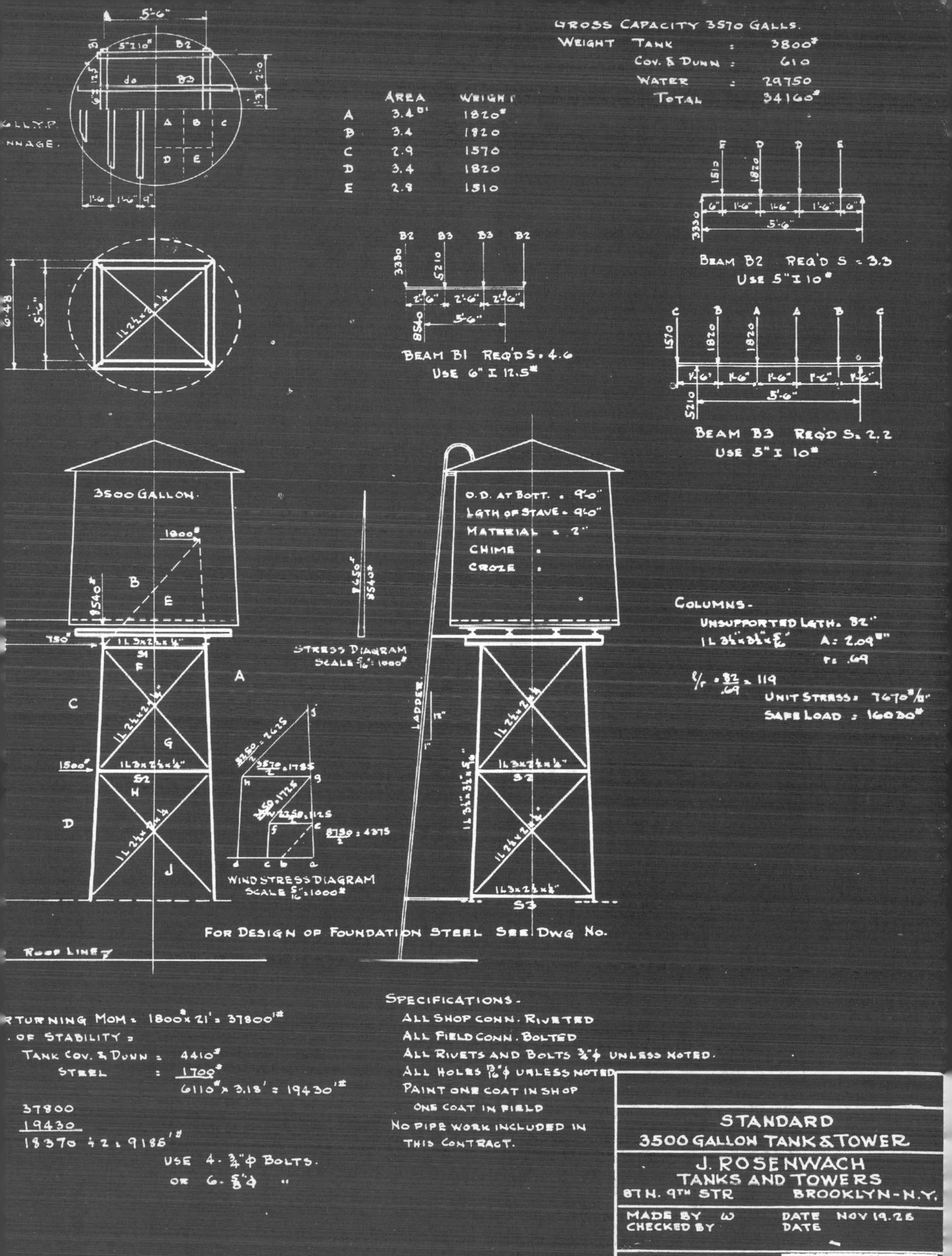

GROSS CAPACITY 3570 GALLS.
WEIGHT TANK : 3800#
COV. & DUNN : 610
WATER : 29750
TOTAL 34160#
AREA WEIGHT
A 3.4 1820#
B 3.4 1820
C 2.9 1570
D 3.4 1820
E 2.8 1510
BEAM B1 REQ'D S. 4.6
USE 6" I 12.5#
BEAM B2 REQ'D S = 3.3
USE 5" I 10#
BEAM B3 REQ'D S. 2.2
USE 5" I 10#
3500 GALLON.
O.D. AT BOTT. = 9'-0"
LGTH OF STAVE = 9'-0"
MATERIAL = 2"
CHIME
CROZE
STRESS DIAGRAM
SCALE 5/16" = 1000#
WIND STRESS DIAGRAM
SCALE 5/16" = 1000#
LADDER
COLUMNS -
UNSUPPORTED LGTH. 82"
A: 2.09
UNIT STRESS = 7670
SAFE LOAD = 16030#
FOR DESIGN OF FOUNDATION STEEL SEE DWG NO.
ROOF LINE
RTURNING MOM = 1800# x 21' = 37800'#
. OF STABILITY =
TANK COV. & DUNN = 4410#
STEEL : 1700#
6110# x 3.18' = 19430'#
37800
19430
18370 ÷ 2 = 9185'#
USE 4 - 3/4" ϕ BOLTS.
OR 6 - 5/8" ϕ "
SPECIFICATIONS -
ALL SHOP CONN. RIVETED
ALL FIELD CONN. BOLTED
ALL RIVETS AND BOLTS 3/4" ϕ UNLESS NOTED.
ALL HOLES 13/16" ϕ UNLESS NOTED
PAINT ONE COAT IN SHOP
ONE COAT IN FIELD
NO PIPE WORK INCLUDED IN
THIS CONTRACT.
STANDARD
3500 GALLON TANK & TOWER
J. ROSENWACH
TANKS AND TOWERS
87 N. 9TH STR BROOKLYN-N.Y.
MADE BY W DATE NOV 19.26
CHECKED BY DATE
DRAWING NO. 3.5.B1